D0432491

A JETBLACK SUNRISE

Poems About War and Conflict

Compiled by Jan Mark

Illustrated by John Yates

HODDER
Wayland

Editor: Katie Orchard
Designer: Jane Hawkins

Published in Great Britain in 2003
by Hodder Wayland, an imprint of Hodder Children's Books

The right of Jan Mark to be identified as the compiler and John Yates
as the illustrator of this Work has been asserted by them in
accordance with the Copyright, Designs and Patents Act, 1988.

Cataloguing in Publication Data
A Jetblack Sunrise: Poems about War and Conflict
  (Poetry Powerhouse)
  1. War Poetry 2. Children's Poetry
  I. Mark, Jan
  808.9'19358

ISBN: 0 7502 4293 0

Printed and bound in Great Britain by Clays Limited, St Ives plc.

Hodder Children's Books
A division of Hodder Headline Limited
338 Euston Road, London NW1 3BH

CONTENTS

Foreword

No one expects to read an anthology as they would a novel, starting on page 1 and working through to the end. Nevertheless, anyone compiling an anthology needs some kind of ground plan, and this collection was put together in the form of a novel, in four chapters.

The first begins with pleas for peace – one day, not yet – giving way to the attitudes that lead to conflict, then to the disruption and dislocation at the outbreak of hostilities. In the second section the majority of the poems were written by those who experienced warfare at first hand, either on active service or as civilians, knew its realities, fought, suffered, resisted, died, and saw the end coming exhausted rather than triumphant.

War is not over when it's over. The third section surveys the damage. The dead are at least out of it; but what becomes of the survivors, and how do the living cope with the burdens of remembrance and forgetting? The final section examines an uncomfortable proposition: that war is the normal pursuit of mankind; peace breaks out occasionally.

Each poem, with one or two exceptions, is accompanied by the date on which it was written or published. Look at those dates. The greater number are from the twentieth century, but since humans first invented writing, they have been writing about war.

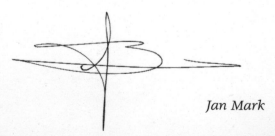

Jan Mark

PEACE IN OUR TIME

Strangest Dream

Last night I had the strangest dream,
I'd never dreamed before;
I dreamed the world had all agreed
To put an end to war.

I dreamed I saw a mighty room,
The room was full of men,
And the paper they were signing said,
They'd never fight again.

And when the paper was all signed
And a million copies made,
They all joined hands and bowed their heads
And grateful prayers were prayed.

And the people in the streets below
Were dancing round and round,
And swords and guns and uniforms
Were scattered on the ground.

Last night I dreamed the strangest dream,
I'd never dreamed before;
I dreamed the world had all agreed
To put an end to war.

Ed McCurdy
1951

Isaiah's Prophecy

In the days to come,
The Mount of the LORD's House
Shall stand firm above the mountains
And tower above the hills;
And all the nations
Shall gaze on it with joy.
And the many peoples shall go and say:
'Come,
Let us go up to the Mount of the LORD,
To the House of the God of Jacob;
That He may instruct us in His ways,
And that we may walk in His paths.'
For instruction shall come forth from Zion,
The word of the LORD from Jerusalem.
Thus He will judge among the nations
And arbitrate for the many peoples,
And they shall beat their swords into ploughshares
And their spears into pruning hooks:
Nation shall not take up
Sword against nation;
They shall never again know war.

An extract from The Book of Isaiah
Probably written around 500CE

Brotherhood

O brother man, fold to thy heart thy brother:
    Where pity dwells the peace of God is there,
To worship rightly is to love each other,
    Each smile a hymn, each kindly deed a prayer.

Follow with reverent steps the great example
    Of him whose holy work was doing good:
So shall the wide earth seem our Father's temple,
    Each loving life a psalm of gratitude.

Then shall all shackles fall: the stormy clangour
    Of wild war music o'er the earth shall cease;
Love shall tread out the baleful fire of anger,
    And in its ashes plant the tree of peace.

J. G. Whittier
Late nineteenth century

Disarmament

One spake amid the nations, 'Let us cease
    From darkening with strife the fair World's light,
We who are great in war be great in peace.
    No longer let us plead the cause by might.'

But from a million British graves took birth
    A silent voice – the million spake as one –
'If ye have righted all the wrongs of earth,
    Lay by the sword! Its work and ours is done.'

John McCrae
1899

Harp Song of the Dane Women

What is a woman that you forsake her,
And the hearth-fire and the home-acre,
To go with the old grey Widow-maker?

She has no house to lay a guest in –
But one chill bed for all to rest in,
That the pale suns and the stray bergs nest in.

She has no strong white arms to fold you,
But the ten-times-fingering weed to hold you –
Out on the rocks where the tide has rolled you.

Yet, when the signs of summer thicken,
And the ice breaks, and the birch-buds quicken,
Yearly you turn from our side, and sicken –

Sicken again for the shouts and the slaughters.
You steal away to the lapping waters,
And look at your ship in her winter-quarters.

You forget our mirth, and talk at the tables,
The kine in the shed and the horse in the stables –
To pitch her sides and go over her cables.

Then you drive out where the storm-clouds swallow,
And the sound of your oar-blades, falling hollow,
Is all we have left through the months to follow.

Ah, what is Woman that you forsake her,
And the hearth-fire and the home-acre,
To go with the old grey Widow-maker?

Rudyard Kipling
1906

Nationality

I have grown past hate and bitterness,
I see the world as one;
Yet, though I can no longer hate,
My son is still my son.
    All men at God's round table sit,
    And all men must be fed;
    But this loaf in my hand,
    This loaf is my son's bread.

Mary Gilmore
c. 1960

11

Big Steamers

'Oh, where are you going to, all you Big Steamers,
With England's own coal, up and down the
    salt seas?'
'We are going to fetch you your bread and
    your butter,
Your beef, pork, and mutton, eggs, apples,
    and cheese.'

'And where will you fetch it from, all you
    Big Steamers,
And where shall I write you when you
    are away?'
'We fetch it from Melbourne, Quebec,
    and Vancouver –
Address us at Hobart, Hong-Kong, and Bombay.'

'But if anything happened to all you Big Steamers,
And suppose you were wrecked up and down the
    salt sea?'
'Then you'd have no coffee or bacon for breakfast,
And you'd have no muffins or toast for your tea.'

'Then I'll pray for fine weather for all you
    Big Steamers,
For little blue billows and breezes so soft.'
'Oh, billows and breezes don't bother Big Steamers,
For we're iron below and steel-rigging aloft.'

'Then I'll build a new lighthouse for all you
   Big Steamers,
With plenty wise pilots to pilot you through.'
'Oh, the Channel's as bright as a ball-room already,
And pilots are thicker than pilchards at Looe.'

'Then what can I do for you, all you Big Steamers,
Oh, what can I do for your comfort and good?'
'Send out your big warships to watch your
   big waters,
That no one may stop us from bringing
   you food.

'For the bread that you eat and the biscuits
   you nibble,
The sweets that you suck and the joints that you carve,
They are brought to you daily by all us
   Big Steamers –
And if anyone hinders our coming you'll starve!'

Rudyard Kipling
World War I

Mort Aux Chats

There will be no more cats.
Cats spread infection,
cats pollute the air,
cats consume seven times
their own weight in food a week,
cats were worshipped in
decadent societies (Egypt
and Ancient Rome), the Greeks
had no use for cats. Cats
sit down to pee (our scientists
have proved it). The copulation
of cats is harrowing; they
are unbearably fond of the moon.
Perhaps they are all right in
their own country but their
traditions are alien to ours.
Cats smell, they can't help it,
you notice it going upstairs.
Cats watch too much television,
they can sleep through storms,
they stabbed us in the back
last time. There have never been
any great artists who were cats.
They don't deserve a capital C
except at the beginning of a sentence.
I blame my headache and my
plants dying on to cats.

Our district is full of them,
property values are falling.
When I dream of God I see
a Massacre of Cats. Why
should they insist on their own
language and religion, who
needs to purr to make his point?
Death to all cats! The Rule
of Dogs shall last a thousand years!

Peter Porter
1972

The Megalomaniac

Well, bark, ye dogs: I'll bridle all your tongues,
And bind them close with bits of burnish'd steel,
Down to the channels of your hateful throats,
And, with the pains my rigour shall inflict,
I'll make ye roar, that earth may echo forth
The far-resounding torments ye sustain;
As when an herd of lusty Cimbrian bulls
Run mourning round about the females' miss,
And, stung with fury of their following,
Fill all the air with troublous bellowing.
I will, with engines never exercis'd,
Conquer, sack, and utterly consume
Your cities and your golden palaces,
And, with the flames that beat against the clouds,
Incense the heavens and make the stars to melt,
As if they were the tears of Mahomet
For hot consumption of his country's pride;
And, till by vision or by speech I hear
Immortal Jove say, 'Cease, my Tamburlaine,'
I will persist a terror to the world,
Making the meteors that, liked armed men,
Are seen to march upon the towers of heaven,
Run tilting round about the firmament,
And break their burning lances in the air,
For honour of my wondrous victories.

Christopher Marlowe
(An extract from the play Tamburlaine)
1587

Russians

How silly that soldier is pointing his gun at the wood:
he doesn't know it isn't any good.
You see, the cold and cruel northern wind
has frozen the whole battalion where they stand.

That's never a corporal: even now he's frozen
you can see he's only a commercial artist
whom they took and put these clothes on,
and told him he was one of the smartest.

Even now they're in ice it's easy to know
what a shock it's been, a long shock,
coming home to them wherever they go
with their mazed minds taking stock.

Walk among the innocuous parade
and touch them if you like, they're properly stayed:
keep out of their line of sight and they won't look.
think of them as waxworks, or think they're struck

with a dumb immobile spell
to wake in a hundred years with the merry force
of spring upon them in the harmless world. Well,
at least don't think what happens when it thaws.

Keith Douglas
1940

Stormy Day

O look how the loops and balloons of bloom
Bobbing on long strings from the finger-ends
And knuckles of the lurching cherry-tree
Heap and hug, elbow and part, this wild day,
Like a careless carillon cavorting;
And the beaded whips of the beeches splay
And dip like anchored weed round a drowned rock,
And hovering effortlessly the rooks
Hang on the wind's effrontery as if
On hooks, then loose their hold and slide away
Like sleet sidewards down the warm
      swimming sweep
Of wind. O it is a lovely time when
Out of the sunk and rigid sumps of thought
Our hearts rise and race with new sounds and sights
And signs, tingling delightedly at the sting
And crunch of springless carts on gritty roads,
The caught kite dangling in the skinny wires,
The swipe of a swallow across the eyes,
Striped awnings stretched on lawns. New things
      surprise
And stop us everywhere. In the parks
The fountains scoop and flower like rockets
Over the oval ponds whose even skin
Is pocked and goosefleshed by their niggling rain
That frocks a naked core of statuary.

And at jetty's jut, roped and ripe for hire,
The yellow boats lie yielding and lolling,
Jilted and jolted like jellies. But look!
There! Do you see, crucified on palings,
Motionless news-posters announcing
That now the frozen armies melt and meet
And smash? Go home now, for, try as you may,
You will not shake off that fact today.
Behind you limps that dog with tarry paw,
As behind him, perfectly-timed, follows
The dumb shadow that mimes him all the way.

W. R. Rodgers
1940

I'll Make a Man of You

The Army and the Navy need attention,
The outlook isn't healthy you'll admit,
But I've got a perfect dream of a new recruiting
  scheme,
Which I think is absolutely it.
If only other girls would do as I do
I believe that we could manage it alone,
For I turn all suitors from me but the sailor and
  the Tommy,
I've an army and a navy of my own.

On Sunday I walk out with a Soldier,
On Monday I'm taken by a Tar,
On Tuesday I'm out with a baby Boy Scout,
On Wednesday a Hussar;
On Thursday I gang oot wi' a Scottie,
On Friday, the Captain of the crew;
But on Saturday I'm willing, if you'll only take
  the shilling,
To make a man of any one of you.

I teach the tenderfoot to face the powder,
That gives an added lustre to my skin,
And I show the raw recruit how to give
  a chaste salute,
So when I'm presenting arms he's falling in.
It makes you almost proud to be a woman,
When you make a strapping soldier of a kid.
And he says 'You put me through it and I didn't
  want to do it
But you went and made me love you so I did.'

On Sunday I walk out with a Bo'sun,
On Monday a Rifleman in green,
On Tuesday I choose a 'sub' in the 'Blues',
On Wednesday a Marine;
On Thursday a Terrier from Tooting,
On Friday a Midshipman or two,
But on Saturday I'm willing, if you'll only
  take the shilling,
To make a man of any one of you.

Recruiting song from World War I

Who's for the Game?

Who's for the game, the biggest that's played,
    The red crashing game of a fight?
Who'll grip and tackle the job unafraid?
    And who thinks he'd rather sit tight?

Who'll toe the line for the signal to 'Go!'?
    Who'll give his country a hand?
Who wants a turn to himself in the show?
    And who wants a seat in the stand?

Who knows it won't be a picnic – not much –
    Yet eagerly shoulders a gun?
Who would much rather come back with a crutch
    Than lie low and be out of the fun?

Come along, lads – but you'll come on all right –
    For there's only one course to pursue,
Your country is up to her neck in a fight,
    And she's looking and calling for you.

Jessie Pope
World War I

The Drum

    I hate that drum's discordant sound,
    Parading round, and round, and round:
    To thoughtless youth it pleasure yields,
    And lures from cities and from fields,
    To sell their liberty for charms
    Of tawdry lace, and glittering arms;
    And when Ambition's voice commands,
To march, and fight, and fall, in foreign lands.

    I hate that drum's discordant sound,
    Parading round, and round, and round:
    To me it talks of ravaged plains,
    And burning towns, and ruined swains,
    And mangled limbs, and dying groans,
    And widows' tears, and orphans' moans;
    And all that Misery's hand bestows,
To fill the catalogue of human woes.

John Scott
1782

Channel Firing

That night your great guns, unawares,
Shook all our coffins as we lay,
And broke the chancel window-squares,
We thought it was the Judgement-day

And say upright. While drearisome
Arose the howl of wakened hounds:
The mouse let fall the altar-crumb,
The worms drew back into the mounds,

The glebe cow drooled. Till God called, 'No;
It's gunnery practice out at sea
Just as before you went below;
The world is as it used to be:

'All nations striving strong to make
Red war yet redder. Mad as hatters
They do no more for Christés sake
Than you who are helpless in such matters.

'That this is not the judgement-hour
For some of them's a blessed thing,
For if it were they'd have to scour
Hell's floor for so much threatening ...

'Ha, ha. It will be warmer when
I blow the trumpet (if indeed
I ever do; for you are men,
And rest eternal sorely need).'

So down we lay again. 'I wonder,
Will the world ever saner be,'
Said one, 'than when He sent us under
In our indifferent century!'

And many a skeleton shook his head.
'Instead of preaching forty year,'
My neighbour Parson Thirdly said,
'I wish I had stuck to pipes and beer.'

Again the guns disturbed the hour,
Roaring their readiness to avenge,
As far inland as Stourton Tower,
And Camelot, and starlit Stonehenge.

Thomas Hardy
April 1914

The Ballad of Purchase Money

O meet it is and passing sweet
    To live in peace with others,
But sweeter still and far more meet
    To die in war for brothers.

To live is rich; 'tis mean to die
    While English air costs naught.
But breath is base as death is high,
    When England's to be bought.

– And so the lads went out from home
    To wear away in war.
And passed from sight of home: and some
    From sunshine evermore.

Wilfred Owen
1915

Canoe

Well, I am thinking this may be my last
summer, but cannot lose even a part of
pleasure in the old-fashioned art of
idleness. I cannot stand aghast

at whatever doom hovers in the background;
while grass and buildings and the somnolent river,
who know they are allowed to last for ever,
exchange between them the whole subdued sound

of this hot time. What sudden fearful fate
can deter my shade wandering next year
from a return? Whistle and I will hear
and come another evening, when this boat

travels with you alone towards Iffley:
as you lie looking up for thunder again,
this cool touch does not betoken rain;
it is my spirit that kisses your mouth lightly.

Keith Douglas
1940
(He was killed in action four years later.)

Naming of Parts

To-day we have naming of parts. Yesterday,
We had daily cleaning. And to-morrow morning,
We shall have what to do after firing. But to-day,
To-day we have naming of parts. Japonica
Glistens like coral in all of the neighbouring gardens,
    And to-day we have naming of parts.

This is the lower sling swivel. And this
Is the upper sling swivel, whose use you will see,
When you are given your slings. And this is the
  piling swivel,
Which in your case you have not got. The branches
Hold in the gardens their silent, eloquent gestures,
    Which in our case we have not got.

This is the safety-catch, which is always released
With an easy flick of the thumb. And please do not
  let me
See anyone using his finger. You can do it quite easy
If you have any strength in your thumb. The blossoms
Are fragile and motionless, never letting anyone see
      Any of them using their finger.

And this you can see is the bolt. The purpose of this
Is to open the breech, as you see. We can slide it
Rapidly backwards and forwards: we call this
Easing the spring. And rapidly backwards and forwards
The early bees are assaulting and fumbling the flowers:
      They call it easing the Spring.

They call it easing the Spring: it is perfectly easy
If you have any strength in your thumb: like the bolt,
And the breech, and the cocking-piece, and the point
  of balance,
Which in our case we have not got; and the
  almond-blossom
Silent in all of the gardens and the bees going
  backwards and forwards,
      For today we have naming of parts.

Henry Reed
1946

About Being a Member of Our Armed Forces

Remember the early days of the phony war
when men were zombies and women were CWACs
and they used wooden rifles on the firing range?
Well I was the sort of soldier you couldn't trust
with a wooden rifle
and when they gave me a wooden bayonet
life was fraught with peril for my brave comrades
including the sergeant-instructor
I wasn't exactly a soldier tho
only a humble airman
who kept getting demoted
                 and demoted
                         and demoted
to the point where I finally saluted civilians
And when they trustingly gave me a Sten gun

Vancouver should have trembled in its sleep
for after I fired a whole clip of bullets
at some wild ducks under Burrard Bridge
(on guard duty at midnight)
they didn't fly away for five minutes
trying to decide if there was any danger
Not that the war was funny
I took it and myself quite seriously
the way a squirrel in a treadmill does
too close to tears for tragedy
too far from the banana peel for laughter
and I didn't blame anyone for being there
that wars happened wasn't anybody's fault then

Now I think it is

Al Purdy
1968

At Parting

Since we through war awhile must part
Sweetheart, and learn to lose
Daily use
Of all that satisfied our heart:
Lay up those secrets and those powers
Wherewith you pleased and cherished me these
  two years:

Now we must draw, as plants would,
On tubers stored in a better season,
Our honey and heaven;
Only our love can store such food.
Is this to make a god of absence?
A new-born monster to steal our sustenance?

We cannot quite cast out lack and pain.
Let him remain – what he may devour
We can well spare:
He never can tap this, the true vein.
I have no words to tell you what you were,
But when you are sad, think, Heaven could give
  no more.

Anne Ridler
1943

The Silver Tassie

Go fetch to me a pint o' wine,
    An' fill it in a silver tassie;
That I may drink, before I go,
    A service to my bonnie lassie.
That boat rocks at the pier o' Leith,
    Fu' loud the wind blaws frae the ferry,
The ship rides by the Berwick-law,
    And I maun leave my bonnie Mary.

The trumpets sound, the banners fly,
    The glittering spears are rankéd ready;
The shouts o' war are heard afar,
    The battle closes thick and bloody;
But it's no the roar o' sea or shore
    Wad mak me langer wish to tarry;
Nor shout o' war that's heard afar,
    It's leaving thee, my bonnie Mary.

Robert Burns
1788
(Burns did not see active service.)

God is on My Side

Truly, who is a god except the LORD,
    who is a rock but our God? –
    the God who girded me with might,
    who made my way perfect;
    who made my legs like a deer's,
    and let me stand firm on the heights;
    who trained my hands for battle;
    my arms can bend a bow of bronze.
You have given me the shield of Your protection;
    Your right hand has sustained me,
    Your care has made me great.
You have let me stride on freely;
    my feet have not slipped.
I pursued my enemies and overtook them;
    I did not turn back till I destroyed them.
I struck them down,
    and they could rise no more;
    they lay fallen at my feet.
You have girded me with strength for battle,
    brought my adversaries low before me,
    made my enemies turn tail before me;
    I wiped out my foes.

They cried out, but there was none to deliver;
    cried to the LORD, but He did not answer them.
I ground them fine as windswept dust;
    I trod them flat as dirt of the streets.

David, King of Israel (From Psalm 18)
c. 1000CE

The Dilemma

God heard the embattled nations sing and shout
'Gott strafe England!' and 'God save the King!'
God this, God that, and God the other thing –
'Good God!' said God, 'I've got my work cut out.'

J. C. Squire
1915

THE DOGS OF WAR

The Lieutenant of Horse Artillery

Full tilt for my Emperor and King, I
galloped down the moonlit roads of Hungary
past poplar after Lombardy poplar tree
in our dear multicultural Empi-

re alas! on a horse I didn't know
had been requisitioned from a circus. Without fail
he leaped every tree-shadow lying like a fox's tail
over the road, O despite whip, despite Whoa!

unswerving, he hurdled them. My leather
  shako jerked,
my holster slapped my hip, my despatch case too,
every leap! I was clubbed black and blue
inside my tight trousers. So many shadows lurked

to make him soar and me cry out, taking wing
every fifty metres the length of a desperate ride
for my Emperor and King, as our Empire died
with its dream of happy cultures dancing in a ring.

Les Murray
1991
*(The joint monarchy of Austria-Hungary – 1867 –
did not survive World War I.)*

War Game

When the soldiers lost their limbs
They were turned to wounded soldiers

Put to nursing, a farmyard milkmaid
Carried in her pails the limbs of soldiers

A section of the rails was missing: here
The track blew up, hurting the soldiers

A general might have to ride a hippo
Commandeered from Noah's Ark

A wooden tiger carry off the wounded
The milkmaid and her pails as well

The more things went to pot
The more authentic the whole thing got.

D. J. Enright
1973

Address Before Battle to Heavily-outnumbered Troops

If we are mark'd to die, we are enow
To do our country loss; and if to live,
The fewer men, the greater share of honour.
God's will! I pray thee, wish not one man more.
By Jove, I am not covetous for gold,
Nor care I who doth feed upon my cost;
It earns me not if men my garments wear;
Such outward things dwell not in my desires:
But if it be a sin to covet honour,
I am the most offending soul alive.
No, faith, my coz, wish not a man from England:
God's peace! I would not lose so great an honour
As one man more, methinks, would share from me,
For the best hope I have. O do not wish one more!
Rather proclaim it, Westmoreland, through my host,
That he which hath no stomach for this fight,
Let him depart; his passport shall be made,
And crowns for convoy put into his purse:
We would not die in that man's company
That fears his fellowship to die with us.
This day is call'd the feast of Crispian:
He that outlives this day, and comes safe home,
Will stand a tip-toe when this day is nam'd,
And rouse him at the name of Crispian.
He that shall see this day, and live old age,
Will yearly on the vigil feast his neighbours,
And say, 'To-morrow is Saint Crispian':

Then will he strip his sleeve and show his scars,
And say, 'These wounds I had on Crispin's day'.
Old men forget; yet all shall be forgot,
But he'll remember with advantages
What feats he did that day. Then shall our names,
Familiar in his mouth as household words,
Harry the king, Bedford and Exeter,
Warwick and Talbot, Salisbury and Gloucester,
Be in their flowing cups freshly remember'd.
This story shall the good man teach his son;
And Crispin Crispian shall ne'er go by,
From this day to the ending of the world,
But we in it shall be remembered;
We few, we happy few, we band of brothers;
For he to-day that sheds his blood with me
Shall be my brother; be he ne'er so vile
This day shall gentle his condition:
And gentlemen in England now a-bed
Shall think themselves accurs'd they were not here,
And hold their manhoods cheap whiles any speaks
That fought with us upon Saint Crispin's day.

William Shakespeare
1599
(From Henry V, Act IV scene iii: *this speech is delivered
by the king before the Battle of Agincourt in 1415.)*

As the Team's Head-brass

As the team's head-brass flashed out on the turn
The lovers disappeared into the wood.
I sat among the boughs of the fallen elm
That strewed the angle of the fallow, and
Watched the plough narrowing a yellow square
Of charlock. Every time the horses turned
Instead of treading me down, the ploughman leaned
Upon the handles to say or ask a word,
About the weather, next about the war.
Scraping the share he faced towards the wood,
And screwed along the furrow till the brass flashed
Once more.

      The blizzard felled the elm whose crest
I sat in, by a woodpecker's round hole,
The ploughman said. 'When will they take it away?'
'When the war's over.' So the talk began –
One minute and an interval of ten,
A minute more and the same interval.
'Have you been out?' 'No.' 'And don't want to,
  perhaps?'
'If I could only come back again, I should.
I could spare an arm. I shouldn't want to lose
A leg. If I should lose my head, why, so,
I should want nothing more ... Have many gone
From here?' 'Yes.' 'Many lost?' 'Yes, a good few.

Only two teams work on the farm this year.
One of my mates is dead. The second day
In France they killed him. It was back in March,
The very night of the blizzard, too. Now if
He had stayed here we should have moved the tree.'
'And I should not have sat here. Everything
Would have been different. For it would have been
Another world.' 'Ay, and a better, though
If we could see all all might seem good.' Then
The lovers came out of the wood again:
The horses started and for the last time
I watched the clods crumble and topple over
After the ploughshare and the stumbling team.

Edward Thomas
May 1916

43

Boots
(Infantry Columns)

We're foot – slog – slog – slog – sloggin' over Africa –
Foot – foot – foot – foot – sloggin' over Africa –
(Boots – boots – boots – boots – movin' up and
   down again!)
    There's no discharge in the war!

Seven – six – eleven – five – nine-an'-twenty mile
   to-day –
Four – eleven – seventeen – thirty-two the day
   before –
(Boots – boots – boots – boots – movin' up and
   down again!)
    There's no discharge in the war!

Don't – don't – don't – don't – look at what's in front
   of you.
(Boots – boots – boots – boots – movin' up an'
   down again);
Men – men – men – men – men go mad with
   watchin' 'em,
    An' there's no discharge in the war!

Try – try – try – try – to think o' something
   different –
Oh – my – God – keep – me from goin' lunatic!
(Boots – boots – boots – boots – movin' up an'
   down again!)
    There's no discharge in the war!

Count – count – count – count – the bullets in the
  bandoliers.
If – your – eyes – drop – they will get atop o' you!
(Boots – boots – boots – boots – movin' up and
  down again) –
      There's no discharge in the war!

We – can – stick – out – 'unger, thirst, an' weariness,
But – not – not – not – not the chronic sight of 'em –
Boots – boots – boots – boots – movin' up an'
  down again,
      An' there's no discharge in the war!

'Tain't – so – bad – by – day because o' company,
But night – brings – long – strings – o' forty
  thousand million
Boots – boots – boots – boots – movin' up an'
  down again.
      There's no discharge in the war!

I – 'ave – marched – six – weeks in 'Ell an' certify
It – is – not – fire – devils, dark, or anything,
But boots – boots – boots – boots – movin' up an'
  down again,
      An' there's no discharge in the war!

Rudyard Kipling
Boer War

Actors Waiting in the Wings of Europe

Actors waiting in the wings of Europe
we already watch the lights on the stage
and listen to the colossal overture begin.
For us entering at the height of the din
it will be hard to hear our thoughts, hard to gauge
how much our conduct owes to fear or fury.

Everyone, I suppose, will use these minutes
to look back, to hear music and recall
what we were doing and saying that year
during our last few months as people, near
the sucking mouth of the day that swallowed us all
into the stomach of a war. Now we are in it

and no more people, just little pieces of food
swirling in an uncomfortable digestive journey,
what we said and did then has a slightly
fairytale quality. There is an excitement
in seeing our ghosts wandering

Keith Douglas
March 1944
(Unfinished; the poet died in action on 9th June 1944)

Gassed Last Night

Gassed last night and gassed the night before,
Going to get gassed tonight if we never get gassed
  any more.
When we're gassed we're sick as we can be,
'Cos phosgene and mustard gas is much too much
  for me.
They're warning us, they're warning us,
One respirator for the four of us.
Thank your lucky stars that three of us can run,
So one of us can use it all alone.

Bombed last night and bombed the night before,
Going to get bombed tonight if we never get bombed
  any more.
When we're bombed we're scared as we can be.
God strafe the bombing planes from High Germany.
They're over us, they're over us,
One shell hole for just the four of us,
Thank your lucky stars there are no more of us,
'Cos one of us could fill it all alone.

Trench version of Drunk Last Night
World War I

Assault

Gas!
faces turned,
eyes scanned the sky,
hands feverishly ripped open canisters,
and masks were soon covering faces.
A man choked
as the white cloud,
swirling round him like fog, caught him
unawares.
Then his body flopped over.
Shells floated across
as if suspended by hidden strings,
and then, tired,
they sank earthwards.

A command!
I fixed my bayonet,
scrambled over the open trench
and struggled through
the thick pasty mud.

It was quiet
as we walked
except for the sucking,
groaning, squelching sound
which came from the wet earth
as it tried
to creep into our stockings.
The wind cut me.

Over the wall!
Then a whistle.
'Good luck, mates.'
Mind that hole. Through the wire.
Over the top.
And kill.
'God. This is fun!'

Erno Muller
World War I

Uncle Edward's Affliction

Uncle Edward was colour-blind;
We grew accustomed to the fact.
When he asked someone to hand him
The green book from the window-seat
And we observed its bright red cover
Either apathy or tact
Stifled comment. We passed it over.
Much later, I began to wonder
What curious world he wandered in,
Down streets where pea-green pillar boxes
Grinned at a fire-engine as green;
How Uncle Edward's sky at dawn
And sunset flooded marshy green.
Did he ken John Peel with his coat so green
And Robin Hood in Lincoln red?

On country walks avoid being stung
By nettles hot as a witch's tongue?
What meals he savoured with his eyes:
Green strawberries and fresh red peas,
Green beef and greener burgundy.
All unscientific, so it seems:
His world was not at all like that,
So those who claim to know have said.
Yet, I believe, in war-smashed France
He must have crawled from neutral mud
To lie in pastures dark and red
And seen, appalled, on every blade
The rain of innocent green blood.

Vernon Scannell
1965

The Victory Over Ben Abbad
(An extract)

When they saw what it was that pursued them,
Then they took flight in seven different directions.
This was truly the work of God who turned
Their reward into the reward of idiots.
He tied ropes around their hands,
And cords were bound across their hearts.
Their chariots were their own stumbling-blocks,
And their steeds were like chains on their feet.
He cut them off with the breath of his mouth
As a weaver snaps a cord. He broke them like
  threads.
I saw men of renown bound as prisoners,
And brought in, in fetters, dragged
Before the king. Some lived at his command.
Some at his behest were slain.
I grew weary of seeing the smiting and the smitten,
Bespattered, immersed in the blood of life,
And the sole of the foot that had not yet touched
Ground, now wounded with thorns,
And warriors, stricken, pierced to the death,
Thrown to one side, corpses of the heathen.
On the night of the sixth day we pursued them
Like a ravening bird, like a swarm of bees.
We struck down their mighty men and their king;
Their captains and their servants were dead men.

They were like filth upon the face of the earth,
And their heads were in the dust like dung.
They exchanged their rooms, wide halls,
And porticoes, for the wild woods.
We captured our captors, and those that thought
To destroy us were themselves destroyed.
They imagined that we should be their possession,
But they themselves were possessed by our hands.

Samuel Ha-Nagid
1039
(The poet was commander of the army of Granada, fighting the forces of Seville under Ismail ibn Abbad.)

Translated by David Goldstein

Hear Now the Tale of a Jetblack Sunrise

Hear now the tale of a jetblack sunrise,
Hear of the murder in cold blood of four hundred
  and twelve young men.

Retreating they had formed in a hollow square with
  their baggage for breastworks,
Nine hundred lives out of the surrounding enemy's
  nine times their number was the price they took
  in advance,
Their colonel was wounded and their ammunition
  gone,
They treated for an honourable capitulation,
  received writing and seal, gave up their arms,
  and marched back prisoners of war.

They were the glory of the race of rangers,
Matchless with a horse, a rifle, a song, a supper
  or a courtship,
Large, turbulent, brave, handsome, generous, proud
  and affectionate.
Bearded, sunburnt, dressed in the free costume
  of hunters,
Not a single one over thirty years of age.

The second Sunday morning they were brought
  out in squads and massacred ... it was beautiful
  early summer,
The work commenced about five o'clock and was
  over by eight.

None obeyed the command to kneel,
Some made a mad and helpless rush ... some stood
  stark and straight,
A few fell at once, shot in the temple or heart ... the
  living and dead lay together,
The maimed and mangled dug in the dirt ... the
  new-comers saw them there;
Some half-killed attempted to crawl away,
These were dispatched with bayonets or battered
  with the blunts of muskets;
A youth not seventeen years old seized his assassin
  till two more came to release him,
The three were all torn, and covered with the boy's
  blood.

At eleven o'clock began the burning of the bodies;
And that is the tale of the murder of the four
  hundred and twelve young men,
And that was a jetblack sunrise.

Walt Whitman
1855
*(This is a description of an incident in the war
between Texas and Mexico in 1836.)*

Resistance

The fog rolled through the valley in great force.
The bridge was down, they'd never leave that night.
Once the girl got sticks and made a fire
it was quite snug. McAndrew had his flask.
The old organ took Curly's arpeggios
very decently, and there was trout for supper.
Poor Black thought he heard gunfire, but
he was always hearing things. Owls, yes,
but any guns were in the next valley. Niven
brushed out her hair with her back to the fire
as if she'd always lived there. No one lived there
except the dotty caretaker, and he'd gone
to bed. Rod was telling stories about fog
in that ursa major voice of his, when
Black said 'Listen!' and there were four smart taps
on the French window. The girl swore afterwards
she'd seen a shape, but it was only fog –
the snow would have left footprints. Branches?
Nothing was near. Bats then? Scrabbling
was not the sound, it was knuckles on glass.
'I tell you—' Black began, but the macabre
is of limited interest, like far-off gunfire,
and this is not a ghost story. Curly thought
the glass was cracking in unaccustomed heat
from the fire; Rod said it was the organ.
They laughed, and wrestled on the sheepskin.

At first light they all left for the next valley,
blowing on their hands. 'Snowshoes!' the girl cried,
but there was no one listening, in that wind.
So they found out nothing of the stranger
who tapped the glass at dark and disappeared.
They missed the code. They walked right into it.

Edwin Morgan
1983

Napoleon

'What is the world, O soldiers?
          It is I:
I, this incessant snow,
  This northern sky;
Soldiers, this solitude
  Through which we go
          Is I.'

Walter de la Mare
1906

*(Napoleon's attempt to conquer Russia ended
in his retreat from Moscow in December 1812.
The majority of his troops perished.)*

Brother Fire

When our brother Fire was having his dog's day
Jumping the London streets with millions of tin cans
Clanking at his tail, we heard some shadow say
'Give the dog a bone' – and so we gave him our ours;
Night after night we watched him slaver and
  crunch away
The beams of human life, the tops of topless towers.

Which gluttony of his for us was Lenten fare
Who mother-naked, suckled with sparks, were chill
Though dandled on a grill of sizzling air
Striped like a convict – black, yellow and red;
Thus we were weaned to knowledge of the Will
That wills the natural world but wills us dead.

O delicate walker, babbler, dialectician Fire,
O enemy and image of ourselves,
Did we not on those mornings after the All Clear
When you were looting shops in elemental joy
And singing as you swarmed up city block and spire,
Echo your thought in ours? 'Destroy! Destroy!'

Louis MacNeice
November, 1942
*(The poet served as a fire-watcher during
the London Blitz in World War II.)*

For Johnny

Do not despair
For Johnny-head-in-air;
He sleeps as sound
As Johnny underground.

Fetch out no shroud
For Johnny-in-the-cloud;
And keep your tears
For him in after years.

Better by far
For Johnny-the-bright-star,
To keep your head,
And see his children fed.

John Pudney
1941
(The poet served with the RAF in World War II.)

An Irish Airman Forsees His Death

I know that I shall meet my fate
Somewhere among the clouds above;
Those that I fight I do not hate,
Those that I guard I do not love;
My country is Kiltartan Cross,
My countrymen Kiltartan's poor,
No likely end could bring them loss
Or leave them happier than before.
Nor law, nor duty bade me fight,
Nor public men, nor cheering crowds,
A lonely impulse of delight
Drove to this tumult in the clouds;
I balanced all, brought all to mind,
The years to come seemed waste of breath,
A waste of breath the years behind
In balance with this life, this death.

W. B. Yeats
1919
(He did not fly, or see active service in World War I.)

The Death of the Ball Turret Gunner

From my mother's sleep I fell into the State
And I hunched in its belly till my wet fur froze.
Six miles from earth, loosed from its dream of life,
I woke to black flak and the nightmare fighters.
When I died they washed me out of the turret with
   a hose.

Randall Jarrell
1945
(He served with the US Air Force.)

Tank Men

Spruce men wearing khaki drill,
Sunburnt, lean, and trim.
Lithe as whipcord.
Supple as steel.
Hardened thirties, gay nineteens.
Men with tremendous pride
And contempt for other men.
The men of the Tanks.

Storming Valhalla in Shermans.
Charging to Glory in Churchills.

Students, clerks, and plumbers,
Sharing joys and dangers.
Proud heirs to former glories,
The Light Brigade of Forty Three.
Men with tremendous pride
And contempt for other men.
The men of the Tanks.

Storming Valhalla in Shermans.
Charging to Glory in Churchills.

Men who fought and conquered,
Conquered in life and death.
Sweating, working, fighting,
And dying in Tanks.

Youngsters living joyously,
Giving themselves unselfishly.
Men with tremendous pride
And contempt for other men.
The men of the Tanks.

Storming Valhalla in Shermans
Charging to Glory in Churchills.

Trooper Jack Neilson
12 June 1943

Blighters

The House is crammed, tier beyond tier they grin
And cackle at the Show, while prancing ranks
Of harlots shrill the chorus, drunk with din;
'We're sure the Kaiser loves our dear old Tanks!'

I'd like to see a Tank come down the stalls,
Lurching to rag-time tunes, or 'Home, sweet Home',
And there'd be no more jokes in Music-halls
To mock the riddled corpses round Bapaume.

Siegfried Sassoon
February, 1917

Iceland in Wartime

Green and red lights flank the inlet mouth,
As it were a night-club. But three days south,
Below grey Scottish hills, I read a book
About this island, arranged mentally its
  outward look,
Catalogued its properties: sulphur, sagas, geysers
And sphagnum moss; rocks rising in
  snow-ribbed tiers
Over fiords. A slate sky. But now we have arrived
By night, lucky and thankful to have survived,
I was not ready for this blaze of light,
A shield over the harbour, nor the moon like a kite
Tying its lemon rays to the muzzled mountains,
Laying out for inspection what the bay contains:
Destroyers, sweepers, oilers and corvettes.
And there, coming to greet us, the silhouettes
Of launches, their wakes throwing up phosphorus
Like a northern champagne. They'll have sailing
  orders for us:
And before even checking what I imagine
Dawn here to look like, spilling over the snowline
And bald rock the crimson canister of the sun,
We shall be off, the convoy behind us in echelon.

Alan Ross
1952
*(He served in the Royal Navy on Arctic convoys
in World War II.)*

Convoy

Draw the blanket of ocean
Over the frozen face.
He lies, his eyes quarried by glittering fish,
Staring through the green freezing sea-glass
At the Northern Lights.

He is now a child in the land of Christmas:
Watching, amazed, the white tumbling bears
And the diving seal.
The iron wind clangs round the icecaps,
The five-pointed dogstar
Burns over the silent sea,

And the three ships
Come sailing in.

Charles Causley
c. 1950
(He served in the Royal Navy in World War II.)

A Wife in London

I

She sits in the tawny vapour
    That the Thames-side lanes have uprolled,
    Behind whose webby fold on fold
Like a waning taper
    The street-lamp glimmers cold.

A messenger's knock cracks smartly,
    Flashed news is in her hand
    Of meaning it dazes to understand
Though shaped so shortly:
    He – has fallen – in the far South Land …

II

'Tis the morrow; the fog hangs thicker,
    The postman nears and goes:
    A letter is brought whose lines disclose
By the firelight flicker
    His hand, whom the worm now knows:

Fresh – firm – penned in highest feather –
    Page-full of his hoped return,
    And of home-planned jaunts by brake and burn
In the summer weather,
    And of new love that they would learn.

Thomas Hardy
1899
(The Boer War began in this year.)

The Hero

'Jack fell as he'd have wished,' the Mother said,
And folded up the letter that she'd read.
'The Colonel writes so nicely.' Something broke
In the tired voice that quavered to a choke.
She half looked up. 'We mothers are so proud
Of our dead soldiers.' Then her face was bowed.

Quietly the Brother Officer went out.
He'd told the poor old dear some gallant lies
That she would nourish all her days, no doubt.
For while he coughed and mumbled, her weak eyes
Had shone with gentle triumph, brimmed with joy,
Because he'd been so brave, her glorious boy.

He thought how 'Jack', cold-footed, useless swine,
Had panicked down the trench that night the mine
Went up at Wicked Corner; how he'd tried
To get sent home, and how, at last, he died,
Blown to small bits. And no one seemed to care
Except that lonely woman with white hair.

Siegfried Sassoon
August, 1916

*(Sassoon served in the trenches in World War I.
He was awarded the Military Cross, which he
later threw into the River Mersey.)*

Postcards Home

I hold them. Two cards so well preserved
That except for slightly faded ink and sepia
Photographs they could have been written
Last year. Both show Abbeville, the first
Franked Army Post Office, 7 July 1916;
The other, three days later, simply The Somme,
As if it were some holiday resort.
The first seems hurried, nervous.

This is a fine cathedral which you can see
in the distance. The streets are just as narrow
as they look. Dy.

        The second different,
More relaxed.

        My dear little Nancie,
again I am sending you a view of this old town.
I am now on my way back from the front
line. I got all my men there quite safely.
The weather is beautiful but so hot. I have
written a long letter to mother. Hope
you are doing well and have written me a nice
long letter. Love and kisses from Daddy.

Grandfather, I never knew you. You died early.
I think you could have taught me, steadied me.
God knows what you described in that long letter.
I read the cards again, that calm unshaken
Handwriting (for all you knew your final words)
And I wonder what they felt when these came
Through the door. A simple soaring excitement
For the girl, remembered from so far away,
So strong she kept them for sixty-five years.
For the woman a great rinse of relief from
  nightmares
Of mortars and barbed-wire, from the immense
  terrors.
Tears in her room, perhaps, cleaning, then
A letter back.

          Such an ordinary address –
15 Moore Street, South Shore, Blackpool, England.

Christopher Wiseman
1988

Lines for Translation into Any Language

1. I saw that the shanty town had grown over the graves and that the crowd lived among the memorials.

2. It was never very cold – a parachute slung between an angel and an urn afforded shelter for the newcomers.

3. Wooden beds were essential.

4. These people kept their supplies of gasoline in litre bottles, which their children sold at the cemetery gates.

5. That night the city was attacked with rockets.

6. The firebrigade bided its time.

7. The people dug for money beneath their beds, to pay the firemen.

8. The shanty town was destroyed, the cemetery restored.

9. Seeing a plane shot down, not far from the airport, many of the foreign community took fright.

10. The next day, they joined the queues at the gymnasium, asking to leave.

11. When the victorious army arrived, they were
    welcomed by the firebrigade.

12. This was the only spontaneous demonstration
    in their favour.

13. Other spontaneous demonstrations in their
    favour were organised by the victors.

James Fenton
c. 1970
The poet was a freelance reporter in Indo-China
at the end of the Vietnam War.

The Fifth Sense

*A 65-year-old Cypriot Greek shepherd, Nicolis Loizou,
was wounded by security forces early today. He was
challenged twice; when he failed to answer, troops
opened fire. A subsequent hospital examination showed
that the man was deaf.* News item, 30 December 1957.

Lamps burn all the night
Here, where people must be watched and seen,
And I, a shepherd, Nicolis Loizou,
Wish for the dark, for I have been
Sure-footed in the dark, but now my sight
Stumbles among these beds, scattered white boulders,
As I lean towards my far slumbering house
With the night lying upon my shoulders.

My sight was always good,
Better than others. I could taste wine and bread
And name the field they spattered when the harvest
Broke. I could coil in the red
Scent of the fox out of a maze of wood
And grass. I could touch mist, I could touch breath.
But of my sharp senses I had only four.
The fifth one pinned me to my death.

ie soldiers must have called
ie word they needed: Halt. Not hearing it,
was their failure, relaxed against the winter
y, the flag of their defeat.
ith their five senses they could not have told
iat I lacked one, and so they had to shoot.
iey would fire at a rainbow if it had
colour less than they were taught.

irist said that when one sheep
is lost, the rest meant nothing any more.
ere in this hospital, where others' breathing
vings like a lantern in the polished floor
id squeezes those who cannot sleep,
see how precious each thing is, how dear,
ir I may never touch, smell, taste, or see
gain, because I could not hear.

tricia Beer
59

Meeting, 1944
(L.S. and M.S.)

I opened the front door and stood
lost in admiration of
a girl holding a paper box,
and that is how I fell in love.

I've come, she said, *to bring you this,*
some work from the photographer –
or rather it's for a Miss D ...
Would you pass it on to her?

She's my sister, but she's out.
You must wait for her inside.
I'm expecting her right now.
Come in. I held the front door wide.

We talked a little of the war,
of what I did and what she earned;
a few minutes it was, no more,
before my sister had returned.

You're going? Well, I'm off out too.
And so we rose from our two chairs.
I'll be back shortly, Lily dear.
Shall I see you down the stairs?

That's all there is. We met again
until they took the Jews away.
I won't be long. I'll see you soon.
Write often. What else could we say?

I think they were such simple times
we died among simplicities,
and all that chaos seemed to prove
was what a simple world it is

that lets in someone at the door
and sees a pair of lives go down
high hollow stairs into the rain
that's falling gently on the town.

George Szirtes
1986

Road 1940

Why do I carry, she said,
This child that is no child of mine?
Through the heat of the day it did nothing but fidget
  and whine,
Now it snuffles under the dew and the cold star-shine
And lies across my heart heavy as lead,
Heavy as the dead.

Why did I lift it, she said,
Out of its cradle in the wheel-tracks?
On the dusty road burdens have melted like wax,
Soldiers have thrown down their rifles, misers slipped
  their packs:
Yes, and the woman who left it there has sped
With a lighter tread.

Though I should save it, she said,
What have I saved for the world's use?
If it grow to hero it will die or let loose
Death, or to hireling, nature already is too profuse
Of such, who hope and are disinherited,
Plough, and are not fed.

But since I've carried it, she said.
So far I might as well carry it still,
If we ever should come to kindness someone will
Pity me perhaps as the mother of a child so ill,
Grant me even to lie down on a bed;
Give me at least bread.

Sylvia Townsend Warner

Written in Pencil in the Sealed Railway Car

here in this carload
i am eve
with abel my son
if you see my other son
cain son of man
tell him i

Dan Pagis
1972
*(Born in 1930, Pagis was in a concentration camp
during World War II. He escaped in 1944.)*

Translated by Stephen Mitchell

Soldier's Dream

I dreamed kind Jesus fouled the big-gun gears;
And caused a permanent stoppage in all bolts;
And buckled with a smile Mausers and Colts;
And rusted every bayonet with His tears.

And there were no more bombs, of ours or Theirs,
Not even an old flint-lock, nor even a pikel.
But God was vexed, and gave all power to Michael;
And when I woke he'd seen to our repairs.

Wilfred Owen
1917

The Cherry Trees

The cherry trees bend over and are shedding,
On the old road where all that passed are dead,
Their petals, strewing the grass as for a wedding
This early May morn when there is none to wed.

Edward Thomas
May, 1916

Soldiers Plundering a Village

Down the mud road, between tall bending trees,
Men thickly move, then fan out one by one
Into the foreground. Far left, a soldier tries
Bashing a tame duck's head in with a stick,
While on a log his smeared companion
Sits idly by a heap of casual loot –
Jugs splashing over, snatched-up joints of meat.

Dead centre, a third man has spiked a fourth –
An evident civilian, with one boot
Half off, in flight, face white, lungs short of breath.
Out of a barn another soldier comes,
Gun at the ready, finding at his feet
One more old yokel, gone half mad with fear,
Tripped in his path, wild legs up in the air.

Roofs smashed, smoke rising, distant glow of fire,
A woman's thighs splayed open after rape
And lying there still: charred flecks caught in the air,
And caught for ever by a man from Antwerp
Whose style was 'crudely narrative', though 'robust',
According to this scholar, who never knew
What Pieter Snayers saw in 1632.

Anthony Thwaite
c. 1971

All Day it Has Rained ...

All day it has rained, and we on the edge of
  the moors
Have sprawled in our bell-tents, moody and dull
  as boors,
Groundsheets and blankets spread on the muddy
  ground
And from the first grey wakening we have found
No refuge from the skirmishing fine rain
And the wind that made the canvas heave and flap
And the taut wet guy-ropes ravel out and snap.
All day the rain has glided, wave and mist and
  dream,
Drenching the gorse and heather, a gossamer stream
Too light to stir the acorns that suddenly
Snatched from their cups by the wild south-westerly
Pattered against the tent and our upturned
  dreaming faces.
And we stretched out, unbuttoning our braces,
Smoking a Woodbine, darning dirty socks,
Reading the Sunday papers – I saw a fox
And mentioned it in the note I scribbled home; –
And we talked of girls, and dropping bombs
  on Rome,

And thought of the quiet dead and the loud
  celebrities
Exhorting us to slaughter, and the herded refugees;
– Yet thought softly, morosely of them, and as
  indifferently
As of ourselves or those whom we
For years have loved, and will again
Tomorrow maybe love; but now it is the rain
Possesses us entirely, the twilight and the rain.

And I can remember nothing dearer or more to
  my heart
Than the children I watched in the woods on
  Saturday
Shaking down burning chestnuts for the
  schoolyard's merry play,
Or the shaggy patient dog who followed me
By Sheet and Steep and up the wooded scree
To the Shoulder o' Mutton where Edward Thomas
  brooded long
On death and beauty – till a bullet stopped his song.

Alun Lewis
World War II
(Lewis died on active service, in May 1944.)

Spring Will be a Little Late This Year

My soul is scarred with filth of war,
Nerves tremble as stonk falls in distance far.
Gazing over dreary waste of mud,
Broken vines, and shattered homes,
Where simple people lived and children played.
Seeing ever in memory's picture clear,
The burnt out Tanks by Fortunato –
Hearing shells falling on Cherisolo –
And Coriano's scent of death.
Thinking of Springtime, and the Spring Offensive.
With an Eighty-Eight round every bend,
And every mile paid for by a friend.
Spectacular advances for a General's glory
Propped against the toast rack at breakfast,
Newspaper headlines, read by fighting pacifists.
'Only four miles yesterday, My Dear!'
Heedless to the price *we* pay;
Can you blame us if we pray
That spring may be a little late this year.

Trooper Jack Neilson
Written at Ravenna, 26 January 1945
(He served with a tank regiment, the North Irish Horse,
in World War II. Neilson was decorated for gallantry
under fire, receiving the Military Medal and Bar.)

After War

One got peace of heart at last, the dark march over,
And the straps slipped, the warmth felt under roof's
  low cover,
Lying slack the body, let sink in straw giving;
And some sweetness, a great sweetness felt in mere
  living.
And to come to this haven after sorefooted weeks,
The dark barn roof, and the glows and the wedges
  and streaks;
Letters from home, dry warmth and still sure rest
  taken
Sweet to the chilled frame, nerves soothed were so
  sore shaken.

Ivor Gurney
World War I
*(A composer, Gurney was gassed and wounded
as a private on the Western Front.)*

When the War is Over

When the war is over
We will be proud of course the air will be
Good for breathing at last
The water will have been improved the salmon
And the silence of heaven will migrate more
    perfectly
The dead will think the living are worth it we
    will know
Who we are
And we will all enlist again

W. S. Merwin
1967

CASUALTIES

Our Children's Children Will Marvel
(An extract)

Our children's children will marvel,
Leafing the textbook:
"Fourteen – 'Seventeen – 'Nineteen.
How did they live? Poor souls – poor devils!'
Children of a new age will read of battles,
Memorize the names of leaders, orators,
The numbers of the slain,
And dates;
They will not learn how sweet, on the field of battle
   roses smelled,
How clear amid the cannons' voices, rang the
   chirping of martins,
The beauty in those years that was
Life.
Never, never laughed the sun with joy
As on the city laid in ruins,
When people, crawling out of cellars,
Cried out in wonder: 'There is still a sun!'

Ilya Ehrenburg
Kiev, 1919

(*He fought in France in World War I and returned to Kiev on the outbreak of the Bolshevik Revolution in 1917.*)

Translated by Jeannette Eyre

The Man He Killed

'Had he and I but met
By some old ancient inn,
We should have set us down to wet
Right many a nipperkin!

'But ranged as infantry,
And staring face to face
I shot at him as he at me,
And killed him in his place.

'I shot him dead because –
Because he was my foe,
Just so: my foe of course he was;
That's clear enough; although

'He thought he'd 'list, perhaps,
Off-hand like – just as I –
Was out of work – had sold his traps –
No other reason why.

'Yes; quaint and curious war is!
You shoot a fellow down
You'd treat if met where any bar is,
Or help to half-a-crown.'

Thomas Hardy
1902

Bye Bye Black Sheep

Volunteering at seventeen, Uncle Joe
Went to Dunkirk as a Royal Marine
And lived, not to tell the tale.
Demobbed, he brought back a broken 303,
A quiver of bayonets, and a kitbag
Of badges, bullets and swastikas
Which he doled out among warstruck nephews.

With gasflame-blue eyes and dark unruly hair
He could have been God's gift. Gone anywhere.
But a lifetime's excitement had been used up
On his one-and-only trip abroad. Instead,
Did the pools and horses. 'Lash me, I'm bored,'
He'd moan, and use language when Gran
Was out of the room. He was our hero.

But not for long. Apparently he was
No good. Couldn't hold down a job.
Gave the old buck to his Elders and Betters.
Lazy as sin, he turned to drink
And ended up marrying a Protestant.
A regular black sheep was Uncle Joe.
Funny how wrong kids can be.

Roger McGough
1986

Old War-dreams

In midnight sleep of many a face of anguish,
Of the look at first of the mortally wounded, (of that
 indescribable look,)
Of the dead on their backs with arms extended wide,
 I dream, I dream, I dream.

Of scenes of Nature, fields and mountains,
Of skies so beauteous after a storm, and at night the
 moon so unearthly bright,
Shining sweetly, shining down, where we dig the
 trenches and gather the heaps,
 I dream, I dream, I dream.

Long have they pass'd, faces and trenches and
 fields,
Where through the carnage I moved with callous
 composure, or away from the fallen,
Onward I sped at the time – but now of their forms
 at night,
 I dream, I dream, I dream.

Walt Whitman
1865
(During the American Civil War, 1861–1865,
Whitman nursed the wounded on both sides.)

Trains in France

All through the night among the unseen hills
The Trains,
The fire-eyed trains,
Call to each other their wild seeking cry,
And I,
Who thought I had forgotten all the War,
Remember now a night in Camiers,
When, through the darkness, as I wakeful lay,
I heard the trains,
The savage, shrieking trains,
Call to each other their fierce hunting-cry,
Ruthless, inevitable, as the beasts
After their prey.
Made for this end by their creators, they,
Whose business was to capture and devour
Flesh of our flesh, bone of our very bone.
Hour after hour,
Angry and impotent I lay alone
Hearing them hunt you down, my dear, and you,
Hearing them carry you away to die,
Trying to warn you of the beasts, the beasts!
Then, no, thought I;
So foul a dream as this can not be true,
Till, from the silence, broke a trembling roar,

And I hear, far away,
The growling thunder of their joyless feasts –
The beasts had got you then, the beasts, the beasts –
And knew
The nightmare true.

Winifred Holtby
1931

(The poet served in France in World War I with the Women's
Auxiliary Army Corps)

The Field

That's where I saw the Lysander crash,
I tell my son,
when I was about your age.
There were two men in it,
both killed.

But it's flat, he says,
just a flat field.
Where's the hole?

I drive on,
hunched tightly around
that scarred place inside me.

Christopher Wiseman
1988

Gunpowder Plot

For days these curious cardboard buds have lain
In brightly coloured boxes. Soon the night
Will come. We pray there'll be no sullen rain
To make these magic orchids flame less bright.

Now in the garden's darkness they begin
To flower; the frenzied whizz of Catherine-wheel
Puts forth its fiery petals and the thin
Rocket soars to burst upon the steel

Bulwark of a cloud. And then the guy,
Absurdly human phoenix, is again
Gulped by greedy flames: the harvest sky
Is flecked with threshed and glittering golden grain.

'Uncle! A cannon! Watch me as I light it!'
The women, helter-skelter, squealing high,
Retreat; the paper fuse is quickly lit,
A cat-like hiss and spit of fire, a sly

Falter, then the air is shocked with blast.
The cannon bangs, and in my nostrils drifts
A bitter scent that brings the lurking past
Lurching to my side. The present shifts,

Allows a ten-year memory to walk
Unhindered now; and so I'm forced to hear
The banshee howl of mortar and the talk
Of men who died; am forced to taste my fear.

I listen for a moment to the guns,
The torn earth's grunts, recalling how I prayed.
The past retreats. I hear a corpse's sons:
'Who's scared of bangers?' 'Uncle! John's afraid!'

Vernon Scannell
1957
(He was wounded in action in World War II.)

A Much Later Conversation

'Your father –
Did he die in error?'

Well, I suppose you could say that.
He was laid up for several months,
Then they said he was well, and
He went back to work. The next year
He was ill again, and this time he died—

'Yes, but what I mean is—'

Well, a widow's pension wasn't much.
We put it to them that getting gassed
In France had buggered up his lungs.
But the War Office wouldn't wear it,
They observed that the war had been over
For some time ...

'I'm sorry, but I didn't mean—'

Oh yes, we had a priest in,
The first we'd ever seen at close quarters.
He gabbled in Latin,
And no one could understand him.
But at least—

'I'm sorry, but you've misunderstood me.
I was only asking
Did your father die in Eire?'

No, he died in England.
But you're right, it may have been a mistake.

D. J. Enright
1973

The Lament of the Demobilized

'Four years,' some say consolingly. 'Oh well,
What's that? You're young. And then it must have been
A very fine experience for you!'
And they forget
How others stayed behind and just got on –
Got on the better since we were away.
And we came home and found
They had achieved, and men revered their names,
But never mentioned ours;
And no one talked heroics now, and we
Must just go back and start again once more.
'You threw four years into the melting-pot –
Did you indeed!' these others cry. 'Oh well,
The more fool you!'
And we're beginning to agree with them.

Vera Brittain
Date unknown (twentieth century)

Disabled

He sat in a wheeled chair, waiting for dark,
And shivered in his ghastly suit of grey,
Legless, sewn short at elbow. Through the park
Voices of boys rang saddening like a hymn,
Voices of play and pleasure after day,
Till gathering sleep had mothered them from him.

•••

About this time Town used to swing so gay
When glow-lamps budded in the light blue trees,
And girls glanced lovelier as the air grew dim, –
In the old times, before he threw away his knees.
Now he will never feel again how slim
Girls' waists are, or how warm their subtle hands.
All of them touch him like some queer disease.

•••

There was an artist silly for his face,
For it was younger than his youth, last year.
Now, he is old; his back will never brace;
He's lost his colour very far from here,
Poured it down shell-holes till the veins ran dry,
And half his lifetime lapsed in the hot race
And leap of purple spurted from his thigh.

•••

One time he liked a blood-smear down his leg,
After the matches, carried shoulder-high.
It was after football, when he'd drunk a peg,
He thought he'd better join. – He wonders why.
Someone had said he'd look a god in kilts,
That's why; and maybe, too, to please his Meg,
Aye, that was it, to please the giddy jilts
He asked to join. He didn't have to beg;
Smiling they wrote his lie: aged nineteen years.

•••

Germans he scarcely thought of; all their guilt,
And Austria's, did not move him. And no fears
Of Fear came yet. He thought of jewelled hilts
For daggers in plaid socks; of smart salutes;
And care of arms; and leave; and pay arrears;
Esprit de corps; and hints for young recruits.
And soon, he was drafted out with drums and cheers.

•••

Some cheered him home, but not as crowds
   cheer Goal.
Only a solemn man who brought him fruits
Thanked him; and then enquired about his soul.

•••

Now, he will spend a few sick years in institutes,
And do what things the rules consider wise,
And take whatever pity they may dole.
Tonight he noticed how the women's eyes
Passed from him to the strong men that were whole.
How cold and late it is! Why don't they come
And put him into bed? Why don't they come?

Wilfred Owen
World War I

Draft of a Reparations Agreement

All right, gentlemen who cry blue murder as always,
nagging miracle makers,
quiet!
Everything will be returned to its place,
paragraph after paragraph.
The scream back into the throat.
The gold teeth back to the gums.
The smoke back to the tin chimney and further on
  and inside
back to the hollow of the bones,
and already you will be covered with skin and
  sinews and you will live,
look, you will have your lives back,
sit in the living room, read the evening paper.
Here you are. Nothing is too late.
As to the yellow star: immediately
it will be torn from your chest
and will emigrate
to the sky.

Dan Pagis
1972

First World War Poets

You went to the front like sheep
And bleated at the pity of it
In academies that smell of abattoirs
Your poems are still studied

You turned the earth to mud
Yet complain you drowned in it
Your generals were dug in at the rear
Degenerates drunk on brandy and prayer
You *saw* the front – and only bleated
The pity!

You survived
Did you burn your generals' houses?
Loot the new millionaires?
No, you found new excuses
You'd lost an arm or your legs
You sat by the empty fire
And hummed music hall songs

Why did your generals send you away to die?
They saw a Great War coming
Between masters and workers
In their own land
So they herded you over the cliffs to be rid of you
How they hated you while you lived!
How they wept over you once you were dead!

What did you fight for?
A new world?
No – an old world already in ruins!
Your children?
Millions of children died
Because you fought for your enemies
And not against them!

We will not forget!
We will not forgive!

Edward Bond
c. 1980

Epitaph on an Army of Mercenaries

These, in the day when heaven was falling,
    The hour when earth's foundations fled,
Followed their mercenary calling
    And took their wages and are dead.

Their shoulders held the sky suspended;
    They stood, and earth's foundations stay;
What God abandoned, these defended,
    And saved the sum of things for pay.

A. E. Housman
1922

Another Epitaph on an Army of Mercenaries

It is a God-damned lie to say that these
Saved, or knew, anything worth any man's pride.
They were professional murderers and they took
Their blood money and impious risks and died.
In spite of all their kind some elements of worth
With difficulty persist here and there on earth.

Hugh Macdiarmid (in reply to A. E. Housman)
1935

The U-Boat

I am floating by the wrecked U-boat,
naked as a dolphin in the August sun.
I've got away, again, from everyone.
I've moored my raft to the periscope
that stays underwater. On it I keep
my shorts and shoes, and coca-cola,
and a Bavarian girly magazine.
I've become so at-home in the ocean
that I think I must someday drown.
Miles away, on the edge of my hometown,
twin cooling towers fork the sky
where an airship phuts, selling beer.
No-one knows the U-boat is here –
no boats approach these rocks,
no swimmers advance. I don't advertise.
I dive to the conning-tower and enter.
Bubbles speed behind me, above me,
but I am fast. I slide past my friend
the skeleton, until my breath runs low,
then I hit the surface he saw long ago
but never quite saw in the end.

Matthew Sweeney
1989

The Monuments of Hiroshima

The roughly estimated ones, who do not sort well
    with our common phrases,
Who are by no means eating roots of dandelion,
    or pushing up the daisies.

The more or less anonymous, to whom no
    human idiom can apply,
Who neither passed away, or on,
    nor went before, nor vanished on a sigh.

Little of peace for them to rest in, less of them
    to rest in peace:
Dust to dust a swift transition, ashes to ash
    with awful ease.

Their only monument will be of others' casting –
A Tower of Peace, a Hall of Peace, a Bridge of Peace
    – who might have wished for something lasting
Like a wooden box.

D. J. Enright
1956
*(The Japanese city of Hiroshima was destroyed
by an atomic bomb on 6 August 1945.)*

Beach Burial

Softly and humbly to the Gulf of Arabs
The convoys of dead sailors come;
At night they sway and wander in the waters
    far under,
But morning rolls them in the foam.

Between the sob and clubbing of the gunfire
Someone, it seems, has time for this,
To pluck them from the shallows and bury them
    in burrows
And tread the sand upon their nakedness;

And each cross, the driven stake of tidewood,
Bears the last signature of men,
Written with such perplexity, with such
    bewildered pity,
The words choke as they begin –

'*Unknown seaman*' – the ghostly pencil
Wavers and fades, the purple drips,
The breath of the wet season has washed their
    inscriptions
As blue as drowned men's lips,

Dead seamen, gone in search of the same landfall,
Whether as enemies they fought,
Or fought with us, or neither; the sand joins them
  together,
Enlisted on the other front.

El Alamein

Kenneth Slessor
1942

A Private

This ploughman dead in battle slept out of doors
Many a frozen night, and merrily
Answered staid drinkers, good bedmen, and
  all bores:
'At Mrs Greenland's Hawthorn Bush,' said he,
'I slept.' None knew which bush. Above the town
Beyond 'The Drover', a hundred spot the down
In Wiltshire. And where now at last he sleeps
More sound in France – that, too, he secret keeps.

Edward Thomas
1915

Drummer Hodge

I

They throw in Drummer Hodge, to rest
    Uncoffined – just as found:
His landmark is a kopje-crest
    That breaks the veldt around;
And foreign constellations west
    Each night above his mound.

II

Young Hodge the Drummer never knew –
    Fresh from his Wessex home –
The meaning of the broad Karoo,
    The Bush, the dusty loam,
And why uprose to nightly view
    Strange stars amid the gloam.

III

Yet portion of that unknown plain
    Will Hodge for ever be;
His homely Northern breast and brain
    Grow to some Southern tree,
And strange-eyed constellations reign
    His stars eternally.

Thomas Hardy
1899

The Soldier

If I should die, think only this of me:
    That there's some corner of a foreign field
That is for ever England. There shall be
    In that rich earth a richer dust concealed;
A dust whom England bore, shaped, made aware,
    Gave, once, her flowers to love, her ways to roam,
A body of England's, breathing English air,
    Washed by the rivers, blest by suns of home.

And think, this heart, all evil shed away,
    A pulse in the eternal mind, no less
        Gives somewhere back the thoughts by
            England given;
Her sights and sounds; dreams happy as her day;
    And laughter, learnt of friends; and gentleness,
        In hearts at peace, under an English heaven.

Rupert Brooke
1914

Dead Man's Dump (An extract)

Burnt black by strange decay
Their sinister faces lie,
The lid over each eye;
The grass and coloured clay
More motion have than they,
Joined to the great sunk silences.

Here is one not long dead.
His dark hearing caught our far wheels,
And the choked soul stretched weak hands
To reach the living world the far wheels said;
The blood-dazed intelligence beating for light,
Crying through the suspense of the far torturing wheels
Swift for the end to break
Or the wheels to break,
Cried as the tide of the world broke over his sight,
'Will they come? Will they ever come?'
Even as the mixed hoofs of the mules,
The quivering-bellied mules,
And the rushing wheels all mixed
With his tortured upturned sight.

So we crashed round the bend,
We heard his weak scream,
We heard his very last sound,
And our wheels grazed his dead face.

Isaac Rosenberg
1917

110

On Picnics

at the goingdown of the sun
and in the morning
i try to remember them
but their names are ordinary names
and their causes are thighbones
tugged excitedly from the soil
by frenchchildren
on picnics

Roger McGough
1967

For the Fallen

With proud thanksgiving, a mother for her children,
England mourns for her dead across the sea.
Flesh of her flesh they were, spirit of her spirit,
Fallen in the cause of the free.

Solemn the drums thrill: Death august and royal
Sings sorrow up into immortal spheres.
There is music in the midst of desolation
And a glory that shines upon our tears.

They went with songs to the battle, they
  were young,
Straight of limb, true of eye, steady and aglow.
They were staunch to the end against odds
  uncounted,
They fell with their faces to the foe.

They shall grow not old, as we that are left
  grow old:
Age shall not weary them, not the years condemn.
At the going down of the sun and in the morning
We will remember them.

They mingle not with their laughing comrades
  again;
They sit no more at familiar tables of home;
They have no lot in our labour of the day-time;
They sleep beyond England's foam.

But where our desires are and our hopes profound,
Felt as a well-spring that is hidden from sight,
To the innermost heart of their own land they are
  known
As the stars are known to the Night;

As the stars that shall be bright when we are dust,
Moving in marches upon the heavenly plain,
As the stars that are starry in the time of our
  darkness,
To the end, to the end, they remain.

Laurence Binyon
1914

Grass

Pile the bodies high at Austerlitz and Waterloo.
Shovel them under and let me work –
            I am the grass; I cover all.

And pile them high at Gettysburg
And pile them high at Ypres and Verdun.
Shovel them under and let me work.
Two years, ten years, and passengers ask the
    conductor:

            What place is this?
            Where are we now?

            I am the grass.
            Let me work.

Carl Sandburg
1918
(He served in the Spanish-American War of 1898.)

COLD AND CIVIL

The Starved Man

The starved man has always been a popular figure: those familiar eyes huge with suffering, bigger than his belly, his mouth set grim in the sadness. We have always watched the travels of the starved man. The starved man and friends shot one by one in the back of the head, blown over into Cambodian graves. How well he dies, that man – pulled under by the sharks – his old act with the napalm, running screaming into the jungle. No one has ever died in so many places. The starved man goes to India. The starved man in Ethiopia. The adventures of the starved man in Uganda. How the starved man ate dirt. How he was tortured in Chile. The starved man goes to Haiti. No one has ever died as often as the starved man, yet somehow he manages to keep on starving. One day he will be recognized for this great talent of his. One day he will get an award. Ladies and gentlemen, a man you're all familiar with, my good friend, the starved man.

Robert Priest
1984

Epitaph on a Tyrant

Perfection, of a kind, was what he was after,
And the poetry he invented was easy to understand;
He knew human folly like the back of his hand,
And was greatly interested in armies and fleets;
When he laughed, respectable senators burst with
  laughter,
And when he cried the little children died in the
  streets.

W. H. Auden
January 1939

The Combat

It was not meant for human eyes,
That combat on the shabby patch
Of clods and trampled turf that lies
Somewhere beneath the sodden skies
For eye of toad or adder to catch.

And having seen it I accuse
The crested animal in his pride,
Arrayed in all the royal hues
Which hide the claws he well can use
To tear the heart out of the side.

Body of leopard, eagle's head
And whetted beak, and lion's mane,
And frost-grey hedge of feathers spread
Behind – he seemed of all things bred.
I shall not see his like again.

As for his enemy, there came in
A soft round beast as brown as clay;
All rent and patched his wretched skin;
A battered bag he might have been,
Some old used thing to throw away.

Yet he awaited face to face
The furious beast and the swift attack.
Soon over and done. That was no place
Or time for chivalry or for grace.
The fury had him on his back.

And two small paws like hands flew out
To right and left as the trees stood by.
One would have said beyond a doubt
This was the very end of the bout,
But that the creature would not die.

For ere the death-stroke he was gone,
Writhed, whirled, huddled in his den,
Safe somehow there. The fight was done,
And he had lost who had all but won.
But oh his deadly fury then.

A while the place lay blank, forlorn,
Drowsing as in relief from pain.
The cricket chirped, the grating thorn
Stirred, and a little sound was born.
The champions took their posts again.

And all began. The stealthy paw
Slashed out and in. Could nothing save
These rags and tatters from the claw?
Nothing. And yet I never saw
A beast so helpless and so brave.

And now, while the trees stand watching, still
The unequal battle rages there.
The killing beast that cannot kill
Swells and swells in his fury till
You'd almost think it was despair.

Edwin Muir
1949

Post Mortem
After the ending of the Vietnam War

Too soon yet to mourn the fallen city,
Too soon yet to scan the crowded sky,
Too soon yet for pain or pity,
But not too soon to wonder why.
This is no time for overloaded birds,
This is the time to trundle out the words.

Poignant, tragic, shocking, bloody, bitter –
It doesn't greatly matter which you use:
They all read well, sound even better
Spoken gravely on the news.
When all is said, the question still remains
To disconcert the nation's finest brains.

How could a potent giant be so humbled?
The blinded husband was the last to know.
Incredibly the fortress crumbled,
The eagle yielded to the crow.
They had the wealth, they ate their apple-pie,
They should have won: computers cannot lie.

There is no easy way to strike a balance
Between the think-tank and the simple brutes;
Might and military talents
Versus the black pyjama-suits.
Charley was good and better than his word:
No one, it seemed, remembered George the Third.

Roger Woddis
1973

Coming Home

The son they love came home then went away.
They asked him why he cried out every night.
He didn't tell them and he couldn't stay.
They try to reach him but he'll never write.
They lie together now. They sleep apart
And still, in dreams, each breaks the other's heart.

And still, in dreams, he's haunted by a child
That stood a moment, looked into his eyes
Not guessing just how far he was defiled,
As if his combat-jacket were disguise.
Don't let the little bastards get to you.
You know exactly what you have to do.

All wars are guilty of their own remorse
And have it out with us before they end.
Some may be just, no doubt. Of course.
In time your enemy becomes your friend.
But there are debts the future can't reclaim –
To kill a child and not to know its name.

To kill a child that couldn't run away,
That stood a moment after it was shot
With puzzled human eyes as if to say
Like you I was so why now am I not?
Then fell. He shot the mother too.
It seemed exactly what he had to do.

And then it seemed exactly where to be
Was nowhere where he had to think of home,
The horror of all words meant lovingly,
The ignorant kindness everyone had shown.
Not only nightmares slay the innocent
And that's the reason why he came and went.

And that's the reason why this can't go on,
And why it's almost culpable to write,
And why I can't stop thinking of our son
And of how easily we sleep at night,
How in this house if anybody screams
We joke next morning. It was only dreams.

Oh only dreams that simply come and go,
That tell us nothing that we can't forget.
We lie beside each other snugly, two
Such comfortable, cautious parents, yet
There was a child who came and went away.
They said *We love you* but he could not stay.

John Mole
1987

Partition

Unbiassed at least he was when he arrived on
  his mission,
Having never set eyes on this land he was called
  to partition
Between two people fanatically at odds,
With their different diets and incompatible gods.
'Time,' they had briefed him in London, 'is short.
  It's too late
For mutual reconciliation or rational debate:
The only solution now lies in separation.
The Viceroy thinks, as you will see from his letter,
That the less you are seen in his company the
  better,
So we've arranged to provide you with other
  accommodation.
We can give you four judges, two Moslem and
  two Hindu,
To consult with, but the final decision must rest
  with you.'

Shut up in a lonely mansion, with police night
  and day
Patrolling the gardens to keep assassins away,
He got down to work, to the task of settling the fate
Of millions. The maps at his disposal were out
  of date
And the Census Returns almost certainly incorrect,
But there was no time to check them, no time to
  inspect
Contested areas. The weather was frightfully hot,
And a bout of dysentery kept him constantly on
  the trot,
But in seven weeks it was done, the frontiers
  decided,
A continent for better or worse divided.

The next day he sailed for England, where he
  quickly forgot
The case, as a good lawyer must. Return he
  would not,
Afraid, as he told his Club, that he might get shot.

W. H. Auden
1966
(In 1947 the subcontinent of India gained its
independence from the British Empire and
was partitioned into India and Pakistan.)

125

Don't Sing
(for Paddy McAloon)

The first time, we were saying grace when
the bump came right up through the table legs
and jumped a custard-apple out of the fruit bowl.
Maria excused us and even the dogs came running
to the garden to see what had happened.
It was a man. His arms and legs were splayed
into impossible positions and his head was bleeding,
gently, like cracked egg, darkening the ground
to a rich brown. Isabel, bless her, said he looked
as though he were digging for worms, and the dint
was so deep we didn't need to dig a hole, just scrape
the topsoil across to bury him. We were popular
down in the village for weeks after.

The second time wasn't really ours because Giraldo
from the upper slope came down to ask us if
we might look in his pig-hut. He hoped it was
a star and wanted us to share in the good luck.
The roof was completely collapsed. He must
  have landed
straight across the dividing wall and exploded.
The pigs were already more than interested
and I had to forbid all five of the children
from looking. Any kind of burial was impossible
so we agreed that the next time a priest was around
he might say a few words inside the hut, and that
no one would go singing to the soldiers.

Giraldo knew of other stories from further north
where men had burst like melons onto the Chaco
or disappeared without a bubble in the soft sponge
by the river. And it isn't that we don't understand;
we do. It's how to tell the children something else.
Maria told the youngest that the men were plucked
by strong winds while sailing to Europe and one day
we might see boats fall out of the sky too.
But I'm worried about Jose. He's sixteen now
and knows a fairy story when he hears one.
What do I tell him the next time he asks
about the army helicopters heading for the clouds?
Or why the man in the potato patch was stone cold?

Simon Armitage
1989

O What is that Sound

O what is that sound which so thrills the ear
    Down in the valley drumming, drumming?
Only the scarlet soldiers, dear,
    The soldiers coming.

O what is that light I see flashing so clear
    Over the distance brightly, brightly?
Only the sun on their weapons, dear,
    As they step lightly.

O what are they doing with all that gear,
    What are they doing this morning, this morning?
Only their usual manoeuvres, dear,
    Or perhaps a warning.

O why have they left the road down there,
    Why are they suddenly wheeling, wheeling?
Perhaps a change in their orders, dear.
    Why are you kneeling?

O haven't they stopped for the doctor's care,
    Haven't they reined their horses, their horses?
Why, they are none of them wounded, dear,
    None of these forces.

O is it the parson they want, with white hair,
    Is it the parson, is it, is it?
No, they are passing his gateway, dear,
    Without a visit.

O it must be the farmer who lives so near.
    It must be the farmer so cunning, so cunning?
They have passed the farmyard already, dear,
    And now they are running.

O where are you going? Stay with me here!
    Were the vows you swore deceiving, deceiving?
No, I promised to love you, dear,
    But I must be leaving.

O it's broken the lock and splintered the door,
    O it's the gate where they're turning, turning;
Their boots are heavy on the floor
    And their eyes are burning.

W. H. Auden
1932

Your Attention Please

The Polar DEW has just warned that
A nuclear rocket strike of
At least one thousand megatons
Has been launched by the enemy
Directly at our major cities.
This announcement will take
Two and a quarter minutes to make,
You therefore have a further
Eight and a quarter minutes
To comply with the shelter
Requirements published in the Civil
Defence Code – section Atomic Attack.
A specially shortened Mass
Will be broadcast at the end
of this announcement –
Protestant and Jewish services

Will begin simultaneously –
Select your wavelength immediately
According to instructions
In the Defence Code. Do not
Take well-loved pets (including birds)
Into your shelter – they will consume
Fresh air. Leave the old and bed-
ridden, you can do nothing for them.
Remember to press the sealing
Switch when everyone is in
The shelter. Set the radiation
Aerial, turn on the geiger barometer.
Turn off your Television now.
Turn off your radio immediately
The Services end. At the same time
Secure explosion plugs in the ears
Of each member of your family. Take
Down your plasma flasks. Give your children
The pills marked one and two
In the C.D. green container, then put
Them to bed. Do not break
The inside airlock seals until
The radiation All Clear shows
(Watch for the cuckoo in your
perspex panel), or your District
Touring Doctor rings your bell.
If before this, your air becomes
Exhausted or if any of your family
Is critically injured, administer
The capsules marked 'Valley Forge'

(Red Pocket in No. 1 Survival Kit)
For painless death. (Catholics
Will have been instructed by their priests
What to do in this eventuality.)
This announcement is ending. Our President
Has already given orders for
Massive retaliation – it will be
Decisive. Some of us may die.
Remember, statistically
It is not likely to be you.
All flages are flying fully dressed
On Government buildings – the sun is shining.
Death is the least we have to fear.
We are all in the hands of God,
Whatever happens happens by His Will.
Now go quickly to your shelters.

Peter Porter
1961

Talk in the Dark

We live in history, says one.
We're flies on the hide of Leviathan, says another.

Either way, says one,
fears and losses.

And among losses, says another,
the special places our own roads were to lead to.

Our deaths, says one,
That's right, says another,
now it's to be a mass death.

Mass graves, says one, are nothing new.
No, says another, but this time there'll be no graves,
all the dead will lie where they fall.

Except, says one, those that burn to ash.
And are blown in the fiery wind, says another.

How can we live in this fear? says one.
From day to day, says another.

I still want to see, says one,
where my own road's going.

I want to live, says another, but where can I live
if the world is gone?

Denise Levertov
1982

The Station Wife

I

This is me and Anna
In our masks and combat jackets
On the runway and that's
Gas that yellow you can almost
See the edges and the men
Inside it with their hoses laughing
At how silly we looked they said
And looking just as silly I'd say
Like space-invaders in a field
Of mustard Anna says
We all look silly and we'd
All be dead if this was real
Though if we keep prepared
We won't be which is why
We're practising and anyway
It all looks real enough to me
And even Jacqueline admits
To feeling just a little sexy
Taking us with all those men
Behind us and us sort of
Crouching there like that and
Grinning underneath our masks
But what's so really good's
The definition of the edges
Round that yellow cloud
With all the men inside
And them so blurry even Jacqui's
Pleased with how this one came out.

II

This is Sue and Debbie
On the rifle range I
Took it and that's
Greg and Terry lying there
Beside them straightening
Their aim and swapping wives
Said Terry with his other arm
Round Debbie's shoulder
So what next I wondered as
The rounds of ammo thudded into
Mannikins with bullseyes
Where their parts would be
Then all of us ran up and counted
While dummies stood there
With their eyes all dead and staring
Like a seizure and the men exclaiming
Well done girlie with their arms
Around the targets' shoulders begging
Take us take us till I laughed
So much I couldn't get it
In and nor can Trevor
Anymore says Anna but I
Wish I had so you could see
The weird resemblances there were
Between those riddled mannikins
And Greg and Terry.

III

This is Tracy standing by the wire
With cutters for a laugh you
Can't tell which side of the fence
She's on but then what happened is
The reason I can't laugh or tell you
What there is to tell since no one told us
Why the siren why the inner gates
Were closed and why our men
Ran criss-cross in the distance then
Assembled on the runway I
Could just see Trevor Greg
And Terry then a tall guard
Snatched my camera saying
Later love you'll get it back
And there's me wondering
What would I do if this was real
Or if it is this time
And where the children are
And must we stay forever with
These skulls this hardware all
The loveless sexiness of being here
Inside the wire outside
The inner gates where even Paul
Goes running criss-cross at
What secret purposes then
Comes home high to hoist his
Penis up and tell me
Baby take a photograph of that.

John Mole
1987

The Hawk in the Train

Springtime in Cambridgeshire. An elderly Paytrain
Limps across the grey-green fens
Under a leaden sky. I sit beside the window
Trying not to look outside. 'Brandon –'

The guard growls. 'Next stop, Brandon.'
The carriages totter over the rusty points.
The ancient diesel engine shudders
To a halt. No one gets out.

Then a sudden twitter of excitement:
Two young men, each with a falcon on his wrist,
Have climbed aboard. Two kids rush up
To pet the birds – are stopped,

Warned to approach slowly, quietly.
'Then maybe – if you're very careful ...'
Helmeted like medieval knights, the hawks
Accept the tentative, one-fingered strokes

As tribute. One lifts a foot in slow salute
Exposing cruel talons. The children shrink back,
Giggling nervously, and are called back to their seats
By parents anxious at the sight of claw and beak.

Freed, the two men take the empty seats
In front of me. They nod a friendly greeting,
Hoping for a chat. Not native fen-men, obviously.
The two blind hawks sit motionless.

I ask them if they've been to some Country Fair
Demonstrating Falconry (out here, you see,
We're very keen on killing birds). No, no! They're
Both appalled at the use of hawks for blood sports.

No. These birds are working birds, on contract
To the US Air Force Tactical Bombing Wing.
The runways, so they tell me, in the spring
Are plagued by flights of nesting birds.

(This is the Pentagon's nightmare:
A bird flies into the intake of a jet
Taking off *and armed*, and in a flash –
No more eastern England ...)

So these two birds are flown –
Once, twice a week – along the runways.
Airborne deterrence, and it works.
Somewhere behind us, an F1-11

Climbs into the grey sky, heading east.
Hearing the roar, the younger hawk
Jerked from his coma, shrieks:
'A-Wake! A-Wake! A-Wake!'

Mick Gowar
1990

At Lunchtime   A Story of Love

When the busstopped suddenly to avoid
damaging a mother and child in the road, the
younglady in the greenhat sitting opposite
was thrown across me, and not being one to
miss an opportunity i started to makelove
with all my body.

At first she resisted saying that it
was tooearly in the morning and toosoon
after breakfast and that anyway she found
me repulsive. But when i explained that
this being a nuclearage, the world was going
to end at lunchtime, she tookoff her
greenhat, put her busticket in her pocket
and joined in the exercise.

The buspeople, and therewere many of
them, were shockedandsurprised and amused-
andannoyed, but when the word got around
that the world was coming to an end at lunchtime, they put their pride in their pockets
with their bustickets and madelove one with
the other. And even the busconductor, being
over, climbed into the cab and stuck up
some sort of relationshop with the driver.

Thatnight, on the bus coming home,
wewere all alittle embarrassed, especially me
and the young lady in the greenhat, and we
all started to say in different ways howhasty
and foolish we had been. Butthen, always
having been a bitofalad, i stood up and
said it was a pity that the world didn't nearly
end every lunchtime and that we could always
pretend. And then it happened ...

Quick asa crash we all changed partners
and soon the bus was aquiver with white
mothballbodies doing naughty things.

> And the next day
> And everyday
> In everybus
> In everystreet
> In everytown
> In everycountry

people pretended that the world was coming
to an end at lunchtime. It still hasn't.
Although in a way it has.

Roger McGough
1967

Couple Waiting

Leaving the door of the whitewashed house ajar
the man runs to the top of the hill
where he shields his eyes from the evening sun
and scans the sea. Behind him, a woman
holds a curtain back, but when he turns
and shakes his head, she lets the curtain fall.
She goes to the mirror beneath the flag
where she searches her face for signs of
the change her body tells her has begun.
The man shuts the door and sits at the table
where a chicken's bones are spread on two plates.
He thinks of his friends on the Atlantic,
coming up the western coast, laden
with well-wrapped bundles for his stable
that no horse uses. He thinks of his country,
and how his friends and he, with the help
of those bundles, would begin to set it right.
He calls the woman over and feels her stomach,
then asks why she thinks the boat is late.
Like him, she's harassed by an image –
the boat, searchlit, in French or Spanish waters,
guns pointed, a mouth at a megaphone.
Like him, she does not voice her mind,

instead sends him to the hill once more
in the dying light, to watch the red sun
sink in the water that's otherwise bare,
while she sits in the dark room, thinking
of the country their child will grow up in.

Matthew Sweeney
1989

Norn Arln

a wee folla know was kilt
stone dad by there you see
on Bolfost today he wasn't
onvolved if you know whaddamean
jus walkin along this side
the road one day opened fair
withight onny warn atoll
then they wonder whey the
weewons throw stones adam
bleedin bostards

Alan Moore
1986

The Hero
(After W. B. Yeats)

On the Birmingham pub-bombings of
November 21, 1974

I went out to the city streets,
Because a fire was in my head,
And saw the people passing by,
And wished the youngest of them dead,
And twisted by a bitter past
And poisoned by a cold despair,
I found at last a resting-place
And left my hatred ticking there.

When I was fleeing from the night
And sweating in my room again,
I heard the old futilities
Exploding like a cry of pain;
But horror, should it touch the heart,
Would freeze my hand upon the fuse,
And I must shed no tears for those
Who merely have a life to lose.

Though I am sick with murdering,
Though killing is my native land,
I will find out where death has gone,
And kiss his lips and take his hand;
And hide among the withered grass,
And pluck, till love and life are done,
The shrivelled apples of the moon,
The cankered apples of the sun.

Roger Woddis
1974

Anseo

When the Master was calling the roll
At the primary school in Collegelands,
You were meant to call back *Anseo*
And raise your hand
As your name occurred.
Anseo, meaning here, here and now,
All present and correct,
Was the first word of Irish I spoke.
The last name on the ledger
Belonged to Joseph Mary Plunkett Ward
And was followed, as often as not,
By silence, knowing looks,
A nod and a wink, the Master's droll
'And where's our little Ward-of-court?'

I remember the first time he came back
The Master had sent him out
Along the hedges
To weigh up for himself and cut
A stick with which he would be beaten.
After a while, nothing was spoken;
He would arrive as a matter of course
With an ash plant, a salley-rod.
Or, finally, the hazel-wand
He had whittled down to a whip-lash,
Its twist of red and yellow lacquers
Sanded and polished,
And altogether so delicately wrought
That he had engraved his initials on it.

I last met Joseph Mary Plunkett Ward
In a pub just over the Irish border.
He was living in the open,
In a secret camp
On the other side of the mountain.
He was fighting for Ireland,
Making things happen.
And he told me, Joe Ward,
Of how he had risen through the ranks
To Quartermaster, Commandant:
How every morning at parade
His volunteers would call back *Anseo*
And raise their hands
As their names occurred.

Paul Muldoon
1980

The Loneliness of the Military Historian

Confess: it's my profession
that alarms you.
This is why few people ask me to dinner,
though Lord knows I don't go out of my way
  to be scary.
I wear dresses of sensible cut
and unalarming shades of beige,
I smell of lavender and go to the hairdresser's:
no prophetess mane of mine,
complete with snakes, will frighten the youngsters.
If I roll my eyes and mutter,
if I clutch at my heart and scream in horror
like a third-rate actress chewing up a mad scene,
I do it in private and nobody sees
but the bathroom mirror.

In general I might agree with you:
women should not contemplate war,
should not weigh tactics impartially,
or evade the word *enemy*,
or view both sides and denounce nothing.
Women should march for peace,
or hand out white feathers to arouse bravery,
spit themselves on bayonets
to protect their babies,
whose skulls will be split anyway,
or, having been raped repeatedly,
hang themselves with their own hair.

These are the functions that inspire general comfort.
That, and the knitting of socks for the troops
and a sort of moral cheerleading.
Also: mourning the dead.
Sons, lovers, and so forth.
All the killed children.

Instead of this, I tell
what I hope will pass as truth.
A blunt thing, not lovely.
The truth is seldom welcome,
especially at dinner,
though I am good at what I do.
My trade is courage and atrocities.
I look at them and do not condemn.
I write things down the way they happened,
as near as can be remembered.
I don't ask *why*, because it is mostly the same.
Wars happen because the ones who start them
think they can win.

In my dreams there is glamour.
The Vikings leave their fields
each year for a few months of killing and plunder,
much as the boys go hunting.
In real life they were farmers.
They come back loaded with splendour.
The Arabs ride against Crusaders
with scimitars that could sever
silk in the air.

A swift cut to the horse's neck
and a hunk of armour crashes down
like a tower. Fire against metal.
A poet might say: romance against banality.
When awake, I know better.

Despite the propaganda, there are no monsters,
or none that can be finally buried.
Finish one off, and circumstances
and the radio create another.
Believe me: whole armies have prayed fervently
to God all night and meant it,
and been slaughtered anyway.
Brutality wins frequently,
and large outcomes have turned on the invention
of a mechanical device, viz. radar.
True, valour sometime counts for something,
as at Thermopylae. Sometimes being right –
though ultimate virtue, by agreed tradition,
is decided by the winner.
Sometimes men throw themselves on grenades
and burst like paper bags of guts
to save their comrades.
I can admire that.
But rats and cholera have won many wars.
Those, and potatoes,
or the absence of them.
It's no use pinning all those medals
across the chests of the dead.
Impressive, but I know too much.
Grand exploits merely depress me.

In the interests of research
I have walked on many battlefields
that once were liquid with pulped
men's bodies and spangled with exploded
shells and splayed bone.
All of them have been green again
by the time I got there.
Each has inspired a few good quotes in its day.
Sad marble angels brood like hens
over the grassy nests where nothing hatches.
(The angels could just as well be described as *vulgar*
or *pitiless*, depending on camera angle.)
The word *glory* figures a lot on gateways.
Of course I pick a flower or two
from each, and press it in the hotel Bible
for a souvenir.
I'm just as human as you.

But it's no use asking me for a final statement.
As I say, I deal in tactics.
Also statistics:
for every year of peace there have been four hundred
years of war.

Margaret Atwood
1995

Index of First Lines

Index of Authors

Copyright Acknowledgements

The compiler and publishers gratefully acknowledge permission to reproduce the following copyright material:

Anvil Press Poetry for Alan Moore's *Norn Arln* in 'Opia' by Alan Moore (1986)

Barbara Levy Literary Agency, representatives of the Estate of Seigfried Sassoon, for *The Hero* and *Blighters*

Mark Bostridge on behalf of Vera Brittain for *The Lament of the Demobilized*

Carcanet Press Ltd for Hugh Macdiarmid's *Another Epitaph on an Army of Mercenaries* in 'Complete Poems'; Sylvia Townsend Warner for *Road*, in 'Selected Poems' (1985)

Curtis Brown Group Ltd, London on behalf of Margaret Atwood copyright © for *The Loneliness of the Military Historian*

Dunham Literary on behalf of Randall Jarrell as agents for the author's estate, for his poem *Death of the Ball Turret Gunner* © 1945 Randall Jarrell, copyright renewed 1983 by Mary Jarrell

ETT Imprint for Mary Gilmore's *Nationality* from 'Mary Gilmore's Selected Poems' (Sydney 2003)

Faber and Faber Limited for W. H. Auden's *Epitaph on a Tyrant*, *Partition* and *O What is that Sound* in 'The Collected Poems by W. H. Auden' (1976); Keith Douglas' *Russians* © 1940, *Actors Waiting in the Wings of Europe* and *Canoe* in 'The Complete Poems of Keith Douglas' (2000); Edwin Muir's *The Combat* in 'The Oxford Book of English Verse' (1972) from 'The Collected Poems 1921–58' (Faber and Faber); Paul Muldoon's *Anseo* in 'Poems 1968–1983' by Paul Muldoon

Mick Gowar for *The Hawk in the Train*

Harbour Publishing for Al Purdy's *About Being a Member of our Armed Forces* in 'Beyond Remembering, The Collected Poems of Al Purdy' (2000)

Harcourt Inc for Carl Sandburg's *The Grass*, from 'Chicago Poems' by Carl Sandburg, copyright © 1916 by Holt, Rinehart and Winston and renewed in 1944 by Carl Sandburg

David Higham Associates Limited for Charles Causley's *Convoy* in 'Collected Poems', (Macmillan); Louis MacNeice's *Brother of Fire* in 'Collected Poems' (Faber and Faber); Samuel ha-Nagid's *The Victory Over Ben-Abbad*, Translated by David Goldstein in 'The Jewish Poets of Spain' (Penguin, 1971)

Virago Press for Winifred Holtby's *Trains in France*

The Ivor Gurney Society for Ivor Gurney's *After War*

Jewish Publication Society © 1985 for *Isaiah's Prophecy* and *God is on my Side* (Psalm 18) reprinted from 'The Tanakh', used by permission

Alun Lewis for *All Day it has Rained*

The Mariscat Press for Edwin Morgan's *Resistance*

Methuen publishing Limited for Edward Bond's *First World War Poets* in 'Theatre Poems and Songs by Edward Bond' edited by Malcom Hay & Philip Roberts; and for *I'll Make a Man of You* and *Gassed last Night* in 'Oh What a Lovely War' by Theatre Workshop, Charles Chilton and Joan Littlewood

John Mole for *Coming Home* and *The Station Wife*

Les Murray for *The Lieutenant of Horse Artillery*

Oxford University Press for Henry Reed's *Naming of Parts* in 'Collected Poems' by Henry Reed, Oxford (1991); for D. J. Enright's *War Game* in 'The Terrible Shears, Scenes from a Twenties Childhood' (1973); *A Much Later Conversation* in 'The Terrible Shears: Scenes from a Twenties Childhood' (1973), and *The Monuments of Hiroshima* in 'Bread Rather than Blossoms' (1956), all in 'The Collected Poems of D. J. Enright' (OUP and Watson Little Ltd, 1981)

PFD on behalf of James Fenton © 1983 for *Lines for Translation into any Language*; and on behalf of Roger McGough's for his poems *Bye Bye Black Sheep*, *Melting into the Foreground*, *On Picnics*; and *Lunchtime a Story of Love* © 1967 reprinted by permission

Pollinger Ltd for Denise Levertov's *Talk in the Dark* from 'Candles in Babylon' (1982)

Peter Porter for *Mort Aux Chats* and *Your Attention Please*

Robert Priest for *The Starved Man*

Random House Group Limited for Matthew Sweeny's *The U-Boat* and *Couple Waiting* from 'Selected Poems' by Matthew Sweeny published by Jonathan Cape; and for Roger Woddis' *Post Mortem* and *The Hero* from 'The Woddis Collection' by Roger Woddis published by Barrie & Jenkins

About Jan Mark

Jan Mark's first novel, *Thunder and Lightnings*, won the Penguin/Guardian award for unpublished manuscripts in 1974, and was later awarded the Carnegie Medal. Since then, she has won many awards for her novels and short stories for adults and children, including a second Carnegie Medal (for *Handles*) and the Angel literary award for *Zeno Was Here* and for *Feet*. Most recently, *The Eclipse of the Century* was shortlisted for the 2000 Guardian Children's Fiction Prize. A former teacher, Jan now devotes much of her time to running writing workshops for students and teachers.